The Lion and the Mouse

An Aesop's Fable retold by Mark White

Illustrated by Sara Rojo

Raintree

www.raintreepublishers.co.uk
Visit our website to find out
more information about
Raintree books.

To order:
☎ Phone 0845 6044371
🖹 Fax +44 (0) 1865 312263
✉ Email myorders@raintreepublishers.co.uk

Customers from outside the UK please telephone +44 1865 312262

Raintree is an imprint of Capstone Global Library Limited,
a company incorporated in England and Wales having its registered office
at 7 Pilgrim Street, London, EC4V 6LB
– Registered company number: 6695582

Text © 2012 by Picture Window Books
First published in the United Kingdom in paperback in 2013
The moral rights of the proprietor have been asserted.

Art Director: Kay Fraser
Graphic Designers: Emily Harris and Victoria Allen
Production Specialist: Sarah Bennett
Editor: Catherine Veitch
Originated by Capstone Global Library Ltd
Printed and bound in China by Leo Paper Products Ltd

ISBN 978 1 406 24299 7 (paperback)
16 15 14 13 12
10 9 8 7 6 5 4 3 2 1

British Library Cataloguing in Publication Data
A full catalogue record for this book is available
from the British Library.

What is a fable?
A fable is a story that teaches a lesson.
In some fables, animals may talk and
act the way people do. A Greek slave
named Aesop created some of the world's
favourite fables. Aesop's Fables have been
enjoyed for more than 2,000 years.

What happened next?

Read the story to find out...

One afternoon, a mouse set off in search of a snack.

As he walked, the mouse closed his eyes and sniffed. When he opened his eyes again, he was in front of a huge, snoring lion!

The mouse was about to tiptoe away, when
the lion woke up with a great yawn.

The lion caught the mouse under his huge paw. "It looks like I have found a snack," he said.

"Please let me go," begged the mouse.
"I am just a little mouse."

"You are lucky," said the lion. "I am in a good mood. I will give you your freedom."

"Thank you!" the mouse said. "If you ever need my help, I will return the favour."

The lion laughed. "How could you ever help me? Don't worry. You have your freedom. You owe me nothing," he said, walking away.

The mouse went on his way, searching for a snack.

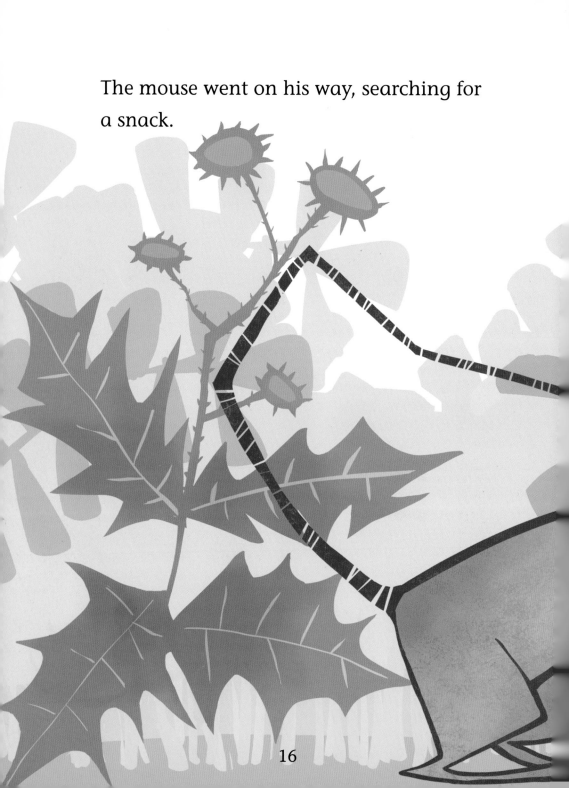

Suddenly, he heard a strange noise.

The mouse followed the noise. He found the lion trapped in a net. "I'll help you!" shouted the mouse.

"What can you do?" asked the lion. "Go away, before you get caught, too!"

But the mouse stayed. He climbed up
the tree and nibbled the net.

His teeth were not as large as the lion's,
but they were very sharp.

Soon the lion was free from the net.

"You helped me when I needed it," the lion said. "I owe you my life."

"Don't worry," said the mouse. "You have your freedom. You owe me nothing."

The new friends walked into the jungle together. "You didn't think I could help you," said the mouse, "but even a small act of kindness is worthwhile."